Them's Good Words, Vol. 1

By Bhudi Lokhuza

Them's Good Words, Vol. 1

by Bhudi Lokhuza

Copyright 2024 by Bhudi Lokhuza

ISBN: 978-0-9825657-3-5

Published in the USA by Them's Good Books.

Dedicated to other people's wives.

This page was intentionally left blank. There's no need to email anyone about it.

Contents

The page was also intentionally left blank. There's still no need to email anyone about it.

This page is not blank. It has two sentences in it.

Dialogue

Much like dialogue in porn, my writing is seldom done well. I write not because I'm good at it but because I'm a storyteller who happens to have a love for writing. Anyone can tell a story. Writing well is another story. My other reason for writing is that it is the second most enjoyable thing I can do by myself—next to sleeping.

Cultivating a Delusion

I watched as she walked away, hating myself for what I'd done to her.

The heels of her feet rolled over the edges of her high-heeled shoes like muffins—dry, cracked muffins no one would ever want.

She walked with pride, her head held high, sure of herself, and ready to take on the world. That was all my fault.

They would never like her, want her, accept her, tolerate her, or give her a chance. They'd claw and shred her into a weeping pile of misery. All of that would be my fault. Where was the line between building self-esteem and cultivating a delusion?

The Game

The game, one they'd played countless times before by defying their parents, started, as usual, the moment their parents' car disappeared down the long driveway, but this time, within seconds, the younger boy was on the floor, twitching as blood trickled from his nose.

Down the Road

Down the road from him, in a brick house with two skeletal brown dogs that looked like strays, lived chubby Sue, whose dimples on her cheeks, showing through her faded jeans, made her the object of his desires.

No Way Forward

She saw no way forward, no way backwards. Her life as she'd known it was coming to an end.

Had she been living in a different century, old-time villagers would have been swarming outside her house, brandishing pitchforks and flaming torches and frothing at the mouth. In this century, however, an avalanche of vitriol came to her phone.

She'd always wanted social media attention and worldwide internet fame, but not this. Soon, the company would be distancing itself from her. Her words would be reposted over and over. No post she'd ever made online would go unscrutinized. After getting fired, the bills would still come.

Eyes Narrowed

E yes narrowed by the midafternoon heat, in the alley behind the restaurants, amidst the stench of discarded food, he stood in the shadow of the building, head tilted to one side, tongue rolling a toothpick in one corner of his mouth. He wiped his hands on his sauce- and flour-stained apron as he contemplated the life he'd imagined and the life he had.

Wide-Eyed

W ide-eyed, on his knees in the back of her closet, he finally discovered why she'd spent twenty years being so protective of that closet. For his mother, the quintessential soccer mom, pairs of seven-inch-high-heeled shoes, the kind favored by bare-chested ladies in certain establishments, would have been difficult to explain.

Average

She stood, looking in the mirror, determined not to cry. "Average" was what they'd called her; average. The most brilliant woman in the building, the most intelligent person in the entire company, was, in their words, average.

They didn't know she'd heard them, both men and women, but more women than men, ganging up on her, piling on behind her back.

She wasn't sure what hurt more—the fact that it was something they all said behind her back or the fact that she knew they were right. Average, unremarkable, nothing spectacular, was what she was. She, the company's vice president, had not been blessed with good looks.

Dubai

Walking in as if he owned the place— because he did—he proclaimed to his minimum wage employees, gathered in the breakroom as they ate their homemade sandwiches, that everyone should spend at least one weekend a month in Dubai.

Remembering the Messages

Remembering the messages she'd read, soon after the quick spurt of rain had stopped, as thin clouds of steam rose from the roadway, she sped down Memory Lane, determined to catch them in the act.

Overrated

She stood next to the crib, scowling at the writhing, squirming mass that, only three days ago, she'd squeezed out of her womb. Limbs jerking, flailing, and occasionally making some semblance of graceful movement, it appeared oblivious of her presence.

She'd read the books, watched the videos, and taken the classes. She'd talked to friends and listened to insufferable in-laws and well-meaning neighbors. Still, she felt none of what they'd described. It wasn't so much that she hated the baby; she felt nothing for the baby.

Motherhood was definitely overrated.

In the Hush That Fell

In the hush that fell across the conference room table, he removed his fedora from his head, examined it as if he had no idea where it had come from, looked back at them, one by one—right in the eyes—and said, "Go ahead. I dare you. I know some guys from Sicily who owe me a favor."

Watching in Silence

Watching in silence, my mind fast-forwarded to a decade in the future, when their boy, Junior, would be a teenager who'd never heard the word "No."

The Train Station

On the anniversary of the day he should have come back home to her, she went to the train station. She went to the station like she had done every year since that day, all dressed up, wearing makeup and in his favorite type of shoes.

At the station, which bustled with activity, she paced leisurely, back and forth, watching the departures and arrivals. She watched as kids shrieked in delight, as hugs were exchanged and kisses were shared.

Everyone had someone to meet, someone to send off, or somewhere to go. That is, everyone except her.

Leaning Back

Leaning back on her chair, she smiled, fighting the urge to let the venomous viper within her come out as she eyed the stack of work her manager had just lumped on the desk.

Shame Fell Over Her

Shame fell over her wrinkled and tired face as she stood hunched over at the checkout line, listening to the impatient grunts and sighs of the customers behind her as her fingers—disfigured by time and arthritis—rummaged in her purse for money she knew wasn't there.

Hate

Hate, she'd been told, was a bad word. She hated her parents for that. She should never feel hate, they'd said. Now, leaning against the kitchen wall, arms across her chest, all grown up, after years of repressing it, here she was, feeling nothing but hate. Some people deserved hatred— intense, palpable, nostril-flaring hatred. The type of hatred that leads to online searches for long, silver-bladed butcher knives, meat cleavers, and wood chippers. That was the type she felt.

She looked at the clock on the microwave, then turned towards the line of recently purchased knives on the magnetic knife holder on the wall next to the kitchen cabinet. He'd be home soon.

She Drove

She drove towards the setting sun, fingers tightly gripping the steering wheel, lips curled and quivering as tears welled in her eyes.

Self-Disclosure

From the amount of self-disclosure she was making, I could tell she was angling for some form of confession from me. The poor girl had no idea who she was dealing with.

They Knew

The realization landed like a cascading, heavy, ice-cold waterfall smashing into her face, stifling her breath, leaving her wondering how she'd failed to see something so obvious. Eyes closed, face buried in her hands, it flashed through her mind—

all of it—the little things, the not-so-little, the now-so-obvious things that made her cringe with shame.

He knew. They all knew, and now she knew they all knew. Pretty soon, strangers on the internet would know.

Her stomach knotted, twisted, and, without warning, vomit spewed across the break room and splashed on the sink, fridge, and cabinets. At any moment, a coworker could walk in, take one look at the mess, and then turn around and leave. Yet another thing everyone would know.

Quietly

Quietly, from a few tables away, I watched her hands gesture animatedly in the almost empty restaurant, her fake-eyelashed eyes sparkling as she spoke to him, her plump lips revealing pearly teeth as she lied to the man she claimed to love.

My Reaction

My reaction was a slight nod as I sat, propping my chin up with my fist, elbow resting on the armrest, desperately fighting the urge to fist pump like someone who'd just won the national lottery.

She Pretended

She pretended not to see him as he stepped into the doorway and stopped. Crossing his arms in front of his chest, he leaned against the door frame, looking at her. She didn't look up. Instead, she continued to lean against the headboard, tapping away on her laptop.

He knew something, she was sure. How much, she wasn't sure.

Thankfully, from where he stood, he couldn't see her fingers trembling on the keyboard or the nonsensical combination of letters she was typing. If she could just remain calm and avoid eye contact, maybe it would all blow over.

The sweat forming on her forehead, probably still not enough for him to notice from the doorway, was becoming a problem. If she wiped it off with the back of her hand, that might draw attention to it. If she left it there, he might eventually notice it.

Standing in That Basement

Standing in that basement, ignoring the smell of stagnant water on an old carpet, he knew he should have felt some guilt, compassion, or remorse, not a gripping, suffocating urge to strip off his clothes and force her to look at him.

It Was Never My Intention

I t was never my intention to eavesdrop, but when you're in an exam room at the doctor's office, and you happen to know the person in the next room, and that person happens to be rumored to have an infection of the nether regions, one's ears tend to perk up involuntarily.

The Handyman

The handyman came early that morning, leaving her on her knees, on the edge of the bed, disappointed but thankful her toys were within reach under the pillow. He said he had other locations to service.

She found herself thinking about his words as his truck crunched its way out on the gravel-covered driveway. He had locations to service, not work, but locations to service. She had never wanted to think about how many other wives received his extra services. Lately, however, she'd found herself thinking more and more about that.

She slid out her toy, flung it onto the bed, and collapsed into a frustrated heap. "Other locations to service" didn't sit well with her.

She Opened Her Eyes

S lowly, she opened her eyes and saw in the darkness, at the foot of her bed, a man silhouetted against the open doorway.

Being of Impeccable Character

B eing of impeccable character, I fully intended to inform her that pressing "delete" on an email didn't necessarily mean that the email was completely gone. I was going to tell her later— maybe—after offering to optimize the virtual work environment on her laptop.

Fridays

I wake up, hearing noises from the apartment below. She's crying again, the way she has every Friday since I moved in. I hear his voice, muffled as always, talking in earnest. Rolling over, I squint at the clock in the darkness. It's a little after three in the morning.

Burying my face in my elbow, I try to fall asleep again. I know it won't work. It never works. I'll lie here, listening to her sobs, wondering what is wrong with her, with him, and how they met.

I've come to hate Fridays. That's when she comes to visit.

Eventually

Eventually, when morning finally came, she woke up to birds singing outside the window, his footsteps down the hallway, and the smell of coffee, eggs, and bacon in the air. Still on her wrists and ankles, on her spread-eagled body: chains.

The Important Thing

The important thing wasn't that my five-year-old self had lied, even though the powers that be disagreed. The important thing was that the family heirloom, one I'd been told to never touch, had been broken, and the cat, at one point, had been seen standing next to it. That was my story. No one could prove otherwise.

The Oak Tree

Her body, prone on the giant oak tree's almost horizontal branch, looked limp, arms and legs dangling, motionless, towards the ground. Her face, on its side, was turned away from me. For a moment, I stood silently, paralyzed by fear.

If she was alive, and I startled her, she could come tumbling down, break her neck, and die. In all likelihood, I'd be a murder suspect. On the other hand, if she were already dead, I'd probably still be a murder suspect. I'd have to explain why I had been out in the woods, by myself, under an oak tree with a dead, naked woman on it.

In the Shower

In the shower, warm water pouring over her head, face, and down the rest of her body, she stood—motionless, sighing, thinking, regretting. Last night had not been a great night.

Smiling at Strangers

There was something about smiling at strangers, no matter how much they smiled at me, that didn't work for me.

Under the Desk

Something—I don't know what—told me not to make a sound. When they entered, I was on my back on the floor at the rear of the classroom, removing gum from under the desk—punishment for sticking gum under the desk.

I could only see them from their feet up to their knees. For a moment or two, I couldn't quite place his brown pants and giant black shoes; then, it came to me. On the other hand, her legs, immediately recognizable beneath her knee-length skirt, were as familiar to me as her rear end, which I couldn't see at that moment.

The door clicked shut. The lights went off. Moans and kisses followed before pants and panties hit the floor.

Under the Blazing Sun

Under the blazing sun, in a sweltering parking lot, a collective gasp went through the crowd as feet shuffled while necks, glistening with sweat, extended for a better view.

The Two Best Employees

Upon hearing that, as the two best employees, they'd have to stay late and grind, a momentary glint flashed across their faces, further cementing my long-held suspicion that their spouses were not being taken for a ride. The ride was elsewhere.

The Brain

Her face is a picture of agony. She is sitting in the middle of the floor in my kitchen. The bases of her palms press against her temples as if trying to prevent her head from exploding. Looking up at me, red-eyed, she asks me to help her. I tell her I'll do all I can.

She tells me she is sorry and says I was right. She tells me that, back then, she knew that I loved her.

Face contorted, she cries, telling me she'd told herself I wasn't exciting enough, didn't party enough, and didn't know how to enjoy life. That's why she'd chosen him instead. He threw the best parties and had the best drugs.

She closes her eyes tightly, opens them, and asks me if her brain is melting. Pounding her temples with the

base of her palms, she asks me if I can hear the voices.
I pull out my phone, telling her I'll call an ambulance.

We wait as I look at her, knowing how much I care for
her, wishing her well, and knowing that I will never
again be able to love her.

On the Edge of the Bed

He sat on the edge of the bed in his underwear,
batting his eyelids like a first grader who'd
just wet his pants in front of the class. Fat
chicks weren't supposed to have better cardio fitness
than he had.

At the New Girl's Desk

At the new girl's desk, making no attempt
whatsoever to be a snoop, I noted with mild
interest that her collection of souvenirs
precisely matched the destinations our overlord had
visited for business.

Caregivers

Eyes filled with dread, the old man, hunched
over his walker, in boxer shorts and no shirt,
shuffles down the hallway towards the
bathroom. His lips are curled in determination and

desperation. He fears he won't make it, but what he fears even more are the repercussions.

The man who fought two wars, now with the body of a starving prisoner of war, is now living in fear, never knowing which caregiver will be coming to his home. With arthritic fingers, barely able to curl around his walker's handles, he feels himself get weaker. Arms and legs that once won weightlifting bets in the gym, now wrinkled and wilted, now nothing more than thin flesh on brittle bone, begin to tremble.

Just as the caregiver's car drives up outside, his bowels, thanks to an antibiotic that helps him stay alive, let him down—draining down his left leg.

There is no knock; the front door opens. They never knock, not even the good ones.

She Held Her Breath

She held her breath, momentarily wrestling with the foolishness of sneaking into a hermit's makeshift cabin deep in the woods. Slowly, she opened the door and froze mid-step when the hinges creaked. Then, on a sunny afternoon without a cloud in the sky, a flash of light, the brightest she'd ever seen— brighter than the sun—bathed everything around her. A searing pain speared its way from the base of her skull to the middle of her right eye. Rather gently, her legs melted, allowing the rest of her body to sway briefly as if in a graceful ballroom dance. She felt her body waft in the air, back and forth, as if caught in a gentle breeze. Finally, as if in the arms of a gentle giant, her body descended to the ground.

As Was Usually the Case

As was usually the case at that time of day, the cool, relaxing breeze was the same, as were the birds chirping in the trees and the scent drifting from the flowers, but none of that mattered without him by her side.

Feeble

Biting her lip and wringing her hands, she sat in her car in the school parking lot, watching her son make his way to the building. His twisted knees pointed towards each other, and his crutches swung wildly as he walked, head jerking forward with each step.

Last night's conversation, as it had done countless times since then, replayed in her mind.

Abruptly, she stops tucking in her son. In a voice as sharp as the glare in her eyes, she asks him why he wants to know what "feeble-minded" means.

Unaccustomed to such a response from her, her son cowers, shuts down, and says nothing more.

Instinctively, she knows where he heard it from—school. She knows who it was directed towards—her son. She is convinced she knows who is behind it all; that sweet-smiling, two-faced swine of a teacher.

She sits in her car, watching her son as he makes his way into the building.

Composure

With the composure of a solemn nun, while still on the bus, she reread the text, knowing that as soon as she got home, she'd twerk like a stripper in front of a professional athlete.

The Envelope

In a crevice between two dusty, cracked floorboards in one of the bedrooms in the abandoned house, she found what looked like it used to be a blue envelope, faded by time, addressed in handwriting that resembled how people wrote when her grandparents were children.

The Roof

She waited until after her husband had left for work before changing out of her sweatpants into tight, see-through, black leggings that showed her red thong. Striking a few poses in front of the mirror, she tilted her head from side to side, assessing her assets. The T-shirt, not tight enough, soon found itself on the floor, replaced by a black sports bra.

She parked her toddler in front of the TV. With her flip-flopped, manicured toes, she kicked a few toys in his direction.

Through the back door, she stepped outside, pretending to be engrossed in her phone. Almost immediately, the hammering on the roof of the garage in the backyard stopped.

They were watching.

They Hated Him

They hated him—all of them, especially the women—partly because of his single, debt-free, stress-free, and drama-free life—and partly because they knew he could have any of them.

The Mature Thing

The mature thing would have been to agree with her and move on, but I chose immaturity by agreeing and holding a grudge. I'd make her pay.

The Moment

The moment she lifts the cushion from the recently delivered used couch, her eyes widen in surprise. Setting aside the vacuum cleaner, she picks up the notebook, opens it, and gasps. Mouth agape, she stares at the name on the inside of the cover.

Although the handwriting and the name are proof enough, she can't believe she has, in her hands, the diary of her high school tormentor. Slowly, she closes the book and sits on the couch, knees together, angled to one side, legs crossed at the ankles, a faraway look blanketing her eyes.

Her high school days scroll through her mind, and she relives each instance of ridicule, humiliation, and heartbreak. She hasn't read a single page.

At First

At first, she was just another woman in the produce section, squeezing some lemons for some reason, oblivious of her looks, other customers, or her effect on him.

Computer Illiteracy

Computer illiteracy among coworkers can be both a curse and a blessing when one is constantly asked to look into what's ailing the machine.

The Week

She sat, holding her phone, wishing she had someone to call. For many, the end of this particular week, the last day of the year, was a milestone worthy of celebration. For her, it was just another night of hiding from the world, not daring to be reached, not daring to reach out, but wishing she could.

Not long ago, moving to the big city had been an easy decision as career prospects and endless social opportunities awaited. Now here she was, alone, a bowl of popcorn between her thighs, watching happy people on TV, just twelve months and one date rape later.

Only After We'd Arrived

Only after we'd arrived at the orphanage, taken a guided tour with two nuns, and then had lunch with even more nuns, did I recognize the address. Someone from within those walls had purchased some toys of intimacy from my website.

By Twilight

By twilight, sitting by the fireplace, legs bent at the knees, ankles together, face buried in one hand, she could no longer weep.

Fingers

The minute I step into her office, my heart almost stops. I compose myself, grateful not to have let out an audible gasp. She's standing behind her desk, applying lotion to her hands. Smiling, she thanks me for submitting my résumé for the volunteer position. Passionately opposed to faking smiles, I nod, telling her that, hopefully, I can help the kids. Nodding back, she tells me how much a positive male influence is needed amongst the kids.

She continues to rub her thick, meaty, ruby-nailed fingers together before extending her right hand towards me. Her hand in mine, plump and soft, is still smeary from the lotion. I know that hand. It's on my website, her middle and index fingers spreading apart her labia.

When Their Eyes Met

When their eyes met from across the packed room, they stared at each other as if looking at an old friend, knowing neither had ever seen the other, neither wanting to look away.

Considering

Considering that she'd just introduced him as her husband and what I'd seen on her computer, there was a lot to unpack. I'd have to offer to optimize the virtual work environment on her laptop once again.

The Melt

In more ways than one, she knew her way into a man's heart. She hummed softly to herself, the same way she'd done almost twenty years ago, in her parent's home, the day she made him his first tuna melt sandwich.

The way to a man's heart was through his stomach, her sweet mama had said. As the tuna melt and more had proved, those were words of wisdom. What her sweet mama had never realized was that by teaching her beloved daughter how to cook, she was providing both a beginning and an end.

The heart she'd won with her cooking, she was now going to stop with her cooking.

Under the Canopy

Pausing and lowering their school bags to the ground, the boys gathered under the canopy of the trees, seeking refuge from the summer sun as they smiled, grinned, giggled, and laughed—all except one.

The Seating Arrangement

The moment I saw the seating arrangement she had made at the dining table, my eyes immediately darted in her direction, wondering if she knew what I knew. When our eyes met, I knew we'd be talking about this later. She'd want to know how I'd known, how long I'd known, and why I hadn't mentioned it to her.

Next to the Highway

Next to the highway, at the top of a green hill, stood a mansion with fifteen bedrooms, even more bathrooms, and one mattress on the floor. As far as everyone knew, he lived alone; a confirmed bachelor, they called him. No one visited him, and he visited no one.

As far as he could tell, all the locals knew him, but from a distance. Many envied him, but from a distance, many talked about him but in hushed tones. He was at peace with it all, not troubled at all since no one ever talked about the mattress on the floor or the girl on that mattress on the floor.

Sunset

As the sun, in its golden shimmer, slowly sank behind the distant skyscrapers, as the frazzled and irritable commuters scurried to get home, as the shadows grew longer by the minute, he stood alone, calmly taking it all in, wishing he was a frazzled and irritable commuter with somewhere to go, instead of waiting for another long, lonely, and cold night in the alley.

She Was Shy

She was shy when it was convenient, faking innocence for its rewards, manipulating the manipulators.

The Competition

At times, the competition between the employees reminded me of how a litter of puppies would clamor for attention after seeing me play with one of them.

Flee

In the dim light of the distant street lights, she ran, her eighteen-year-old stout gymnast legs bounding across the abandoned football field. By morning, the whole world would know her name. By noon, it would become a verb and a punch line.

By afternoon, it would be an insult, thrown about to mock and insult others. No one would pay any attention to what she had experienced. Her story would be hijacked and trivialized.

Darkness

On the edge of the bed, hands clasped between her knees, she sat alone, feeling nothing, wanting nothing, except, perhaps, death.

Time, swiftly, not so quietly, and not particularly kind to her, had flown by. How was that even possible? How could a life lived in constant fear, misery, and hidden bruises actually fly by? Somehow, it had. The time to end it all had arrived.

Her cat, Darkness, as dark as the thoughts in her mind, entered the room, looking up at her and meowing as he approached. On any other day, she'd say something in return—anything to acknowledge his presence, show him some affection, and make him feel welcome. Today, however, wasn't just any other day.

Tail quivering, throat purring, the cat nuzzled against her ankles, then meowed some more. If she were to do it—if she were to end it all today—what would become of Darkness? Maybe she could hold on for a little bit longer, put it off for her beloved Darkness. Surely, it wouldn't be that difficult to find a good home for him.

Eyes narrowed, she leaned forward, rested her elbows on her thighs, and buried her face in her hands, sighing deeply. How had it come to this? As far as her legions

of social media fans were concerned, she had it all—
beauty, money, and influence. She was supposed to be
a picture of true happiness. What they didn't know,
what she wouldn't show, was the life after the selfies,
the pain after the selfies, the bruises after the selfies.

Those with true happiness had smiles after their selfies,
laughter after the selfies, and no bruises after their
selfies. She never smiled after her selfies or laughed
after her selfies. Instead, she had tears after her selfies.

Face still buried in her hands, she heard the voice.

"Mom?"

It was the boy, that damn boy. Three years of
motherhood hadn't made things any better. She raised
her head, turning in his direction.

"I'm hungry," the boy said. "Are you okay?" he
continued. "Have you been crying?"

Turning away from him, she leaned towards the head
of the bed and reached under the pillow. She pulled out
a gun, turned towards the boy, and pointed it right
between his eyes.

After the First Date

After the first date, at a restaurant with an uncomfortable array of silverware for one meal, after eating like the lady she thought he wanted to see, she rushed home to eat like the pig she wanted to be.

Raises, Promotions, and Bonuses

While raises, promotions, and bonuses were as elusive as a winning lottery ticket, morale remained high. Torrid office encounters of the intimate kind tend to do that—for a while.

Blue Was His Favorite Color

She turned, head lowered, walking away from him, holding the flowing blue dress around herself. Through her tears, she struggled to find her footing on the uneven path. She dared not look back, not wanting him to see her this way.

This wasn't how it was supposed to end. This wasn't what she'd planned. This wasn't what she'd dreamed of in her yearning for his return. Sleepless nights, endless sighs, tossing, turning, and painful longing—all for this.

The New Girl at the Office

The new girl at the office, a loud and inconsiderate shrew, would have to be eliminated—they knew a guy for that.

Arriving Home After Midnight

Arriving home after midnight, he found his side of the bed taken over by the twins. With three bodies on the bed, facing in three different directions, he turned around, closed the door, and headed for the guest bedroom.

He'd Made No Effort

He'd made no effort to follow her; she could tell. He'd made no effort to console her, not at all. What difference would that have made anyway? His baby, his baby with that… The simple thought of that other woman's name sent her into gagging, breath-stifling sobs.

From further down in front of her, beyond where the path disappeared around the trees, she heard voices. Other park visitors were walking towards her. She couldn't let them see her this way. They could be people she knew who would talk, point, and laugh behind her back. Turning back wasn't an option. There was no way she could look at him. She stopped and attempted to compose herself, one hand still clinging to her blue dress as if it could offer a magical source of strength.

That dress, that blue dress, carefully selected for this day, two years ago, on the day he'd left—was the dress she'd worn at the farewell party. They'd both loved it. Many a time, he'd told her how good she looked in blue. Remembering that, she'd worn it today because blue was his favorite color. At this moment, however, she wasn't sure she could ever wear a blue dress again—because blue was his favorite color.

When He Entered

When he entered the bedroom, she remembered the text messages she didn't want him to see. She reached for her phone and held on to it as if it were an ancient secret artifact with magical powers and answers to all that ails humanity.

Just Before Work

Just before work started, they huddled and, in excited whispers, discussed the latest breaking news. Someone was pregnant but didn't know who the father was.

It Began Innocently

It had begun innocently enough, harmlessly enough, and slowly enough. She'd never imagined it would ever get to this. Yet, here she was, almost naked, on her knees in a cold, dimly lit basement in a city she couldn't name. How far she was from home, she couldn't say. What the address was, she couldn't say. She had allowed this to happen, is all she could think of. All she'd wanted was just some fun on the internet, some excitement, a little flirting, nothing more. Yet, as time progressed, her mind, her body, her entire being, had evolved.

Knowing He Knew

Knowing he knew her secret but was not confronting her about it was now the difficult part—more difficult, in fact, than the lengths she'd gone to hide it from him.

Longest Tenured

Though she was the longest-tenured employee, everything, including the juiciest gossip circulating faster than a celebrity sex tape, always reached her last.

Net Slave

What had been an afterthought, just something to fill in some downtime, became a craving—an insatiable, all-consuming, gut-clawing craving. She wanted more; more time on the net, more time in chat, more time in front of the camera, more of him, whoever he was.

His power, pull, and ability to mesmerize with his words, hypnotic in a unique way, stunned her only after their online sessions had ended. How had she allowed herself to bare her all on video chats to a man who never showed his face? Day after day, as minutes turned to hours, it was the same thing. He'd call, always via video, of course, but blocked his camera with something blue. Before she knew it, at his command, she'd disrobe. Whatever he wanted to be done, she would do. Whatever he wanted to see, he would see. Maybe it was his voice, calming yet commanding, requesting yet demanding.

There was some safety and danger in his ways—some safety and danger she couldn't quite explain, safety and danger she couldn't escape—safety and danger she didn't want to escape.

Now, here she was, alone, almost naked, on her knees in a cold, dimly lit basement, not a victim—yet.

How Heavy?

At the office, though able and willing, though more capable than most, opportunities never came to her, leaving her on the outside, looking in, wondering how heavy an assault rifle was.

Spite

Somehow, just steps from everyone else, in whispers during the office party, pretending to be lovers to spite their respective spouses had seemed like a good idea.

Barefoot After Midnight

The first time I saw her was at three o'clock in the morning, inside a twenty-four-hour grocery store, as she stood in the wine section, barefoot—and alone.

Other than the smiling hippie running the cash register, the place was deserted. In such a situation, most men, I'm sure, would have seen an opportunity for some adventure. I harbored no such thoughts. Being the gentleman that I am, with no ulterior motive whatsoever and not knowing a thing about alcoholic beverages, I approached her to offer my assistance.

A barefoot woman inside a twenty-four-hour grocery store at three o'clock in the morning. What could go wrong?

On Her First Day

On her first day at her new job, she took in the atmosphere and assessed the situation, determining whose job she'd take over first.

The Minute

The minute she joked about fraudsters on the internet, his demeanor changed, almost as if she'd just called his mother a gold-digging slut.

The Vacant Hallway

The drive to that long-vacant house had taken hours. Now, standing in the hallway, jaws clenched, memories flooding back, goose pimples on his arms, he struggled to control his breath, pulse, and the visions in his head.

As the years rolled by, he'd kept the power connected and paid the water bill. He needed the house he hated and the memories he didn't want. It was who he was, what he was, what he'd always be. He saw it all, heard it all, and relived every minute of it right there in that hallway.

Within minutes, lips quivering and eyes fluttering, he knew the time had come. He'd have to turn around and face the four-hour drive. It was time to kill again.

She Went to the Free Clinic

She went to the free clinic and sat amongst the poor, praying that her regular doctor would never know about the infection she was hiding from him—the infection he'd warned her about.

Alone Into the Forest

A s she had done many times before, she ventured alone into the forest, enjoying the fresh spring greenery that stretched in all directions, not realizing that this time, she wasn't alone.

A Weekend from College

S he stopped abruptly, listening intently. She heard it again, clearly human, several feet into the woods alongside the half-dirt, half-gravel road. Her stomach tightening, she clung to the straps of her backpack, frozen in fear. She dared not breathe but quickly realized she had to.

Her car, broken down two and a half miles behind her, could offer no refuge. Grandma's house, still three miles ahead, wasn't any better. Between the two places, nothing but woods and more woods.

Visiting Grandma, who refused to leave her childhood home in the mountains, had seemed like a good break from the usual college routine. It would have done some good for Grandma to see another human being for a change. Whether or not that could still happen was now in doubt.

He Was a Husband

He was a husband in the sense that he was a man with paperwork that said he was married.

Revenge

Laser-focused on revenge, she glared at her wedding picture on her desk, not noticing her ringing phone or her coworkers, who were now staring at her.

The Occasion

The old man's decades of back-breaking labor in the fields, under the blazing sun, unrelenting cold, and driving rain had come to this. Following his wife's death, when his son, his only child, was just three years old, he'd agonized through life to put him through school, all the way to medical school.

Someone had asked, ever so casually, what he would wear for the occasion. He hadn't had the energy to respond. After all, what would have been a good answer to such a question? How do you dress for the day in which your son will be hung?

Functional Standpoint

From a functional standpoint, my behavior served a purpose—unbridled, full-fledged, unapologetic pettiness. I held and will continue to hold my head high.

The Day He Arrived

The day he arrived at his new home, at the dinner table, surrounded by strangers who were now his new family, his adoptive mother called him a greedy little punk who ate like a rabid dog. So began his new life.

The Victim

Wishing it hadn't come to this, she turned back for one last look. The car, a cloud of dust behind it, slowly rumbled into the distance as he drove away from her. It could have been different. She'd hoped it would be different, but as the dust cleared, it clearly wasn't.

It was at that moment—standing in the soft breeze outside her country home, birds whistling in the trees, chickens clucking in the yard—that love turned into sorrow. Sorrow turned into hate, and hate brought with it a raging desire. At that moment, with a fire billowing inside her, she realized she had a side she'd never known before. She would no longer be a victim.

Forgetting

Forgetting that not all prizes were worth the effort, she continued to bask in the idea that they were the contestants and she was the prize.

Opposites

Opposites don't always attract. Sometimes, they repel. Such was the case when they were assigned to work together. She had to destroy him before he destroyed her. Surviving together was not an option.

The Mansion

The deep breath she took to calm her nerves did no such thing. Wondering if she'd made the right decision, she stood, facing the long-abandoned three-story mansion. Once a striking display of luxury and well-kept gardens, it was now a dirty, hollow, neglected shell of its former self.

The windows, yawning in her direction, revealed the darkness within. Together with the gardens and wrought iron fence suffocating in overgrowth, they were enough to keep most people away. She, however, wasn't most people.

She knew the risks involved. She'd tossed and turned in bed, then looked herself directly in the eye in her bathroom mirror, acknowledging the insanity of it all. Still, she'd made this decision. She was going in.

Long After His Retirement

Long after his retirement age, now hunched over by the burdens of life, he continued to rise before the sun and track his way to the warehouse, where, for reasons he could not quite understand, management still let him act as if he was working, allowing him and his wife to afford some canned food.

From Across Town

From across town, she checked her cell phone's security app and found her five-year-old boy and his three-month-old puppy being stalked by a bear in her backyard. The babysitter, her mother-in-law, known for her distressing relationship with adult beverages, was nowhere to be seen.

In The Shadows

He'd been waiting for two hours when he finally saw it with his own eyes. That's when everything changed. He'd known what to expect, at least, in terms of what he'd see. What he hadn't expected was how he'd feel. Standing in the shadows behind the trees, he dared not move lest he announce his presence. The ground, littered with dry leaves, twigs, and small rocks, was his enemy. With one wrong move, the whole thing would be over.

He'd have to wait until they left.

He was at their mercy, not wanting to be there but unable to leave, not wanting to look but unable to look away.

Drained of All Hope

Drained of all hope, she trudged upstairs, headed for the bedroom, each step heavy with disappointment, each breath labored, her life tittering on the thin line between death and vengeance.

The Good News

The good news, which came just as she was about to give up and crawl back to her ex, warranted a celebration. She'd ignore the voice in her head, telling her it was too early to dance under the confetti.

The Heights of Passion

At two o'clock in the morning, fueled by an unrelenting yearning, it had seemed like a good idea. Now, a twelve-hour drive later, nine feet in the air, hands and toes clinging to the plant-covered iron trellis, her views had changed.

Quite clearly, her body told her she was no longer the high school athlete she had once been. Fingers ached, arms trembled, and toes burned from gripping the trellis that rose against the wall to the roof of his house.

His face, eyes wide with horror, flashed before her eyes. He'd find her, she was sure, lifeless, splattered on the brick-paved ground below.

He Sat Among Them

He sat among them, hands deep in the pockets of his trench coat, giving them nothing to read on his face. He avoided eye contact, occasionally tilting his head back to lean against the wall behind him, knowing it wouldn't be long before their lives changed forever.

In the Hallway

In the hallway, standing just inches away from the new supervisor, within striking distance, knowing that everyone in the nearby offices had heard how she'd just been spoken to, she considered a response. The possibilities were there, though none were appealing. A gut-wrenching, heart-clawing response was what she needed. Then, just like that, ideas came to her, dancing down from above like multicolored leaves in the fall.

Night Driving

She sat in pitch darkness on the side of the road, gripping the steering wheel of her stalled car. Being miles from everywhere, she had no cell phone service. The thickness of the woods adjacent to the road might as well have been a rainforest.

Other than how to drive them and add some fuel, she knew nothing about cars. She'd turned off the lights, vaguely recalling something her father had once said about how leaving the lights on, with the engine not running, would drain the battery.

The temperature inside the car dropped quickly and significantly. Would she be able to make it till morning? Even if she did, then what?

Thighs Aching

Thighs aching, chest burning, his face a picture of death, he reached the top of the hill in the deserted and thickly wooded stretch. His thin twelve-year-old body trembled as he struggled to stay on his bike. Seconds later, it appeared, head lowered, hair raised on its back, and a yellow-fanged snarl foaming and drooling to the ground.

In One Corner

In one corner of the cube farm, under a flood of fluorescent light, away from the rows of cubicles, they stood around her, hands cupping steaming mugs of coffee. Smiling, they encouraged her to apply for the promotion but silently wished death to her and her litter of spoiled brats.

The Yellow Rose

She sat on the bed, wearing his shirt, her soul, like the rose in her hand, dying. Just ten days ago, he'd come over, bearing that yellow rose. Had she missed something? Should she have seen the significance of that color? So happy to see him, she'd placed the rose on the nightstand, focused on him, and given him a day neither would soon forget.

How realistic had it been to expect him not to be with other girls while away from her? He had to have been with someone else. How else could the infection be explained?

Still on the bed, wearing his shirt, she placed both hands on her belly, wondering when she'd feel the first kick.

I Insisted

I insisted—with caution, choosing my words with the precision of a contract attorney, not wanting to tell truths that would embarrass her or lies that would embarrass me.

Under The Apple Tree

A few days before her wedding day, she walked out through the back door of her parents' house towards the orchard, knowing the risk she was taking. Reaching the orchard, lost in thought, a deluge of memories swirled in her mind.

All these years later, the tree was still standing. Eyes filling with tears, she looked at the ground beneath that tree.

In a few days, she'd be a married woman. In many people's eyes, she'd finally be a woman. In her eyes, however, she'd become a woman—many years ago—under that apple tree. All these years later, the flame that burned then still burned today, but not for the man she was about to marry.

I Didn't Say Anything

During the entire staff meeting, I didn't say anything, not because I hadn't seen or heard anything, but because I knew she was a lying, instigating skunk, talking herself into a corner she couldn't walk out of—no matter how much she tried to foul up the air around us.

She Cried

She cried, not for herself, but for her little boy, waiting at home, hoping to see his daddy. She made no excuses for herself. As a grown-up, her choices were hers and hers alone. Her mistakes were hers and hers alone. When she made them, she could dig herself out.

What tormented her, shredding her emotionally, was how her choices impacted her little boy.

She could never love the father of her child. Still, in some twisted way, in a way she could never explain, she longed for the father to love his child. But he didn't, he wouldn't, and never would.

They Whizzed Through Traffic

They whizzed through traffic, deep in conversation, gesturing as they spoke, debating critical economic issues such as buying coffee on the way to work versus making coffee at home.

The Body

When the body washed up on that remote section of the riverbank, he was there, alone. She looked so peaceful, as if taking a nap. He looked around. Other than a few birds in the sky, he saw no signs of life. He gasped for breath; his heart pounded; his thoughts spiraled.

He stood, wrestling with reason, fighting logic, slipping from sanity.

Chest heaving, eyes transfixed on the body, he swallowed, wiped his brow, and looked around again—still, no one in sight. It was just him and the body. No one ever would know.

They Had No Grounds

They had no grounds for hating her, but they did—with a smile, the way their kind tended to hate.

She Woke Up

She woke up face up, spread-eagled, shackled to a bed. Through a window on the far side, some light filtered in. The room, not at all familiar to her, appeared to be the inside of a cabin. Scowling, she tried to make sense of it all.

From outside came voices, male voices, none she recognized. The voices, though loud enough to be heard, weren't clear enough to be understood. At first, there had been two before a third joined.

If she were to call for help, they'd hear her quite clearly. The question was, what would happen next?

I Found It Curious

I found it curious, in a somewhat pathological way, that she'd lie about having a peanut allergy but not about her maniacal attraction to her high school students.

Snowed Out

K nee-deep in snow, with no help in sight, he just knew he'd never make it. The cabins, with warmth, food, and cell phones, could save his life. He was close—so close that a yell for help would be heard.

His mouth wouldn't open; his legs wouldn't move.

Head bobbing, body shaking, his insides quivered. All the while, his eyes never left the cabins. Maybe someone would step outside, see him, and rescue him. Maybe, just maybe.

Then, he saw them, in his mind, his young wife and newborn, umbilical cord still intact, stranded in the car, waiting for him to bring some help.

The earth tilted, swung back and forth, and spun—slowly at first, then faster. Darkness followed.

A Slice of Heaven

B illed as a slice of heaven, it wasn't—unless heaven was made of stale thin slices with dead fruit flies stuck on them.

Her Secret

It was her secret, her shame, her pleasure, all rolled into one, keeping her up until just hours before she had to get up and head for work. Sometimes, she wondered how she'd ever face the world if word got out. Addiction, she'd been told, came in many forms. This had to be one of them.

Walking into work, she checked the clock on the wall, the watch on her wrist, and the time on her phone—eight and a half more hours before she could race home and dive in. Maybe she could call in sick tomorrow, giving herself more time for her secret, her shame, and her pleasure—all rolled into one.

A Student of Life

Generally, when asked, he described himself as a student of life, which was a humble way of hiding his status as a college dropout and trust fund kid who traveled the country, sharing his pot with mentally ill homeless vets.

Cow Puppies

Rolling her car to a stop on the side of the road, a bolt of emotion shot through her. Her eyes narrowed and filled with tears as she watched the calves grazing in the field. She'd called them cow puppies once, believing all baby animals were called puppies.

As a little girl, she'd loved to visit Grandpa's farm with Mommy. Because Daddy was always busy at the hospital, he didn't get to go to Grandpa's much. Grandpa needed a lot of help around the house since Grandma had gone to heaven. While Mommy helped Grandpa inside the house, the little girl got to spend time with the farmhands, feeding the cow puppies.

One day, shots rang out—blood everywhere—Mommy and Grandpa went to heaven, and the police took Daddy away.

Years Later

Years later, while there was still some time, but the execution had finally been scheduled, she still hadn't told a soul about how she'd lied to put him on death row.

Silence Without Peace

There was silence, complete silence; silence without peace. Aching and getting weaker, she longed to hear—something, anything, but mostly his voice. She longed for his return, knowing what he would do to her. She longed for him, knowing how much it would hurt. She longed, knowing she'd wish he would just stop.

She longed, knowing that in the midst of it all, in enduring the unforgiving agony, there'd be some human contact. She longed for what would come at the end—food, water, and the ability to sleep.

She waited in silence, complete silence, silence without peace.

Her Questions

Her questions, though pointed, were gentle but critically important, crafted to guide and trap at the same time.

From Behind

He moved softly on the carpeted floor, approaching her from behind. From where she sat at the desk, facing the window, raising her head—even slightly—would let her see his reflection on the glass. Would she scream or be frozen in terror? In either case, at that point, it would be all over. Still, that was a chance he was willing to take. He had to. The urge was beyond his control.

She Regained Consciousness

When she regained consciousness, she was on her side, still in the abandoned factory, unable to move, with the cold concrete floor shooting an ungodly pain into her hip. A mixture of bodily fluids had flowed out of her mouth onto the floor—under her cheekbone all the way to the top of her head.

Across The Bridge

S he shouldn't have let it happen, but the truth was she had. She still wasn't sure how, but she had allowed it to happen. Now, here she was, alone, facing the bridge, fighting through the pitch darkness of the midnight hour, her only light coming from an outdated, dying cell phone.

If she were to turn around now, avoiding the bridge until the early hours of daylight, what kind of mother would that make her? Would her kids be able to sleep through the night without knowing where she was? Were they even asleep right now? If they'd already called the police—hopefully, they hadn't—Child Protective Services would come calling again. She couldn't go through all that. She just couldn't.

She had to face it. There was no way around it. She had to go across that bridge.

Months Later

M onths later, on a quiet Sunday afternoon, while relaxing in her bedroom, she discovered that the fluffy tiger, a birthday gift from a coworker, had a hidden camera.

Up in Years

Up in years, four times heavier than she had been in the prime of her days as a dancer, she wheeled herself to the open second-floor window. Resting her arms on the bottom edge of the rotting wood of the frame, she leaned over, looking outside.

Barefoot kids, dressed in rags, ran around on the dusty unpaved roads, shrieking with joy and laughter, oblivious of the dismal decaying world around them, unaware of the misfortunes life had dealt them.

Across the street, her back leaning against the corner shack, away from the joy and laughter, stood the little girl. As always, she was alone, head tilted to one side, hands fidgeting with her ragged T-shirt that doubled as a dress. The little girl watched as the others played.

As They Walked Around

As they walked around the table, plates in hand, making their food selections, she eyed everyone else's portion sizes to ensure hers were smaller.

Tom

He came out early that night before the sun had quite set. With the shadows of the buildings, it was dark enough. This early, no one would be naked. But he didn't always need them to be naked. They just had to be there, unaware, merely going on with their lives.

Was he making a mistake? The risk was a little higher this early in the evening. Should he have waited instead of taking a chance like this?

Eye Contact

After she put the files on his desk, he looked up and thanked her, startling and confusing her. No one at the office ever looked in her direction, let alone made eye contact and thanked her.

Silence, Sadness, and Fear

In silence, sadness, and fear of the unknown, she sat on the front stoop, watching her dog. Ears slightly perked up, it sat on its hind legs, facing away from the house and down the paved path leading to the main driveway. Unspoken but understood, this had become a daily ritual.

Feeling some movement, she cradled her pregnant belly. Tears, as was usually the case for this part of the day, filled her eyes. With each day that passed grew the possibility that her baby would never know its father. He was out there in the world, risking his life, fighting other people's wars—people who didn't know or care about him.

They sat in silence, sadness, and fear of the unknown, both hoping they would see him approach.

The Branch

The branch cracked; the boy yelled; boy and branch headed to the ground.

Mother, Daughter, and Son Coalition

When the mother, daughter, and son coalition walked into his home office, he looked up, read their faces, and sighed; whatever the argument was, he'd already lost.

How Far Would Be Too Far?

How far would be too far, given how far she'd already gone?

Help

She approached the house, hindered by fear and propelled by an even bigger fear. She knew about him. Everyone in town knew about him; even worse, he knew about her. She'd seen the way he looked at her, heard his comments, and evaded his advances. Now, she had to go to his house and ask for his help. At sixteen, she was old enough to know what he, the most powerful man in town, the only employer, wanted from her. At sixteen, she'd never given anyone what he wanted from her.

Trembling, she crossed the street, wrapping her old coat more tightly around herself. Maybe, just maybe, if she hid her body beneath the coat…

When It Dawned On Her

That's when it dawned on her that the disheveled tramp she'd ignored as she walked up to the mansion was the landowner and not the help.

The Babysitter

Something was a little off. The sign, offering a babysitting job, had been taped to the back of a stop sign at an intersection near a friend's house. Driving to the appointment, she wondered why the flyer had been so far away from the person offering the job. Weren't these types of posts usually found in the same neighborhood where the job was located?

She found it a little odd that a man was making the arrangements for finding a babysitter. Then again, maybe she was old-fashioned. There was no reason to question something like that in modern society, right?

They Milled Around

They milled around among the guests, smiling, dishing out compliments, periodically checking the time, sick to their stomachs of being on their best behavior.

The Strategy

The strategy, devised in the early hours of the morning, was sound, but like most ideas she had at 3:00 a.m., it was reevaluated during breakfast and discarded by 10:00 a.m.

The Light in the Basement

When she woke up, she scowled in the darkness. The clock was missing from the nightstand. The window, letting in some soft moonlight, was the wrong size and on the wrong side of the room. She tried to sit up to get her bearings but immediately fell back. A sharp pain shot down between her shoulder blades. That's when it all came back to her. This wasn't her bedroom. This wasn't her house. She'd followed the light in the basement, and now, here she was.

When It Was Time to Leave

When it was time to leave the restaurant, he appeared to be stalling, mumbling about work and the need to check his phone. His eyes darted from his phone to her face as if checking to see if she believed him.

She Walked In

She walked in with the confidence of a starving stray puppy accustomed to being pummeled by rocks everywhere it went.

Crouched Behind the Bushes

Crouched behind the bushes, clad in camouflage attire, he watched her approach. The secluded and wooded section of the park—as ideal as the bright twinkle in her eyes, the bounce in her step, and even the way the apple crunched between her teeth—gave him a rush he remembered distinctly.

The Smell of the Pages

The smell of the pages, now yellow with age, brought back memories of her days as a little girl. Back then, she spent her afternoons at her small town's library. Her mother, the sole librarian, would let her run to her heart's content between the shelves as long as she wasn't loud. Flipping through the pages took her back to that pivotal afternoon between the bookshelves. That was the day she met the old man she believed to be Father Christmas.

She'd Never Smelled Blood Before

She'd never smelled blood before, but somehow, when she regained consciousness, she immediately knew that's what it was. Still in the car, which was now upside down, she remembered a remote stretch of road, driving, speeding, and being furious, but couldn't remember why. In the distance, a car drove by, water splashing beneath its tires like it had done on Memory Lane. Her arm twitched, and her eyelids grew heavier.

It Could Have Been a Joyful Moment

It could have been a joyful moment when he stepped out of the bedroom, leaving the door open, allowing his dog, tail wagging, to trot into the room and sit on the floor on her side of the bed. She slid between the sheets, turning her body to face the black Lab. Propping her head up with one arm, she reached out with the other to pet the brown-eyed sweetheart. The dog thumped his tail against the floor as she rubbed behind his ears. It was at that moment that the fragrance—a fragrance she knew so well—hit her. The dog had been around her boyfriend's ex.

Disgusted With Herself

Disgusted with herself, she stood up with the dainty grace and softness of a geriatric elephant with arthritic joints.

The Bouquet

The bouquet, colorful and meticulously arranged as it was, did nothing to sway her emotions.

She Stood Backstage

She stood backstage, sweaty palms clutching the neck of the guitar as if it were some upside-down ceremonial sword. The melody from the stage, a reminder of what she was competing against, drifted towards her, stretching and weaving its way into the giggles and snickers that still echoed in her mind from her last performance.

Back at the House

Back at the house, anxious and determined to spice up her style and be noticed, she stretched her newly purchased outfit along the length of the bed. The thin line between sexy and slutty needed further contemplation.

It Wasn't Just a Rough Patch

It wasn't just a rough patch. He was no longer hopeful. Lying naked on a frozen lake in the middle of the night in the dead of winter could bring more warmth and comfort compared to what he had with her.

Had They Known

Had they known the identity of the man with the dull jacket and a face full of despair, every single one of those waitresses would have begged their manager to sit him in their section of the restaurant. Instead, as he crossed the parking lot and approached the restaurant, they gathered, peering through the window, making faces, and giggling about who he'd be assigned to.

Kites

He only flew kites if they had hidden video cameras in them. Quieter than drones but more challenging to direct, they still managed to meet his goals.

Raw

Gritting her teeth in raw, bitter, and festering emotions, she reached over to the nightstand and turned off the light, breaking the knob.

Somehow

Somehow, the big, rugged mountain of a man spoke in a smooth, calm voice more fitting of a hypnotic therapist than a man who looked like he could pick up her Mini Cooper and, with a flick of the wrist, fling it across the parking lot.

She Was One of Those

She was one of those vibrant, high-spirited girls who carried notebooks with hand-drawn flowers on the cover and always had a water bottle that never got empty.

Muffled and Distant

Though muffled and distant, the sounds were distinct enough for him to know he had found them. Still squatting in the bushes, he looked around for the best route to where they were. He took out his phone and checked to ensure the ringer was off before cautiously taking a step, making sure not to step on anything that might startle them.

When He Finished Playing

When he finished playing, he looked up from the keyboard to see his classmates huddled around him, awestruck and nodding their approval. Just as a smile began to creep across his face, she spoke up, declaring—with a wave of the hand and a roll of the eyes—that at her house, they had a real piano, not some cheap piece of plastic from China.

She Smiled—Slightly at First

She smiled—slightly at first, avoiding eye contact, trying not to break into uncontrollable fits of laughter. She failed. I'd made her laugh. I always made her laugh.

Now Towering Above Me

Now towering above me, the pines stood motionless and in silence, as if reaffirming our secret to never speak of what had happened over two decades ago.

She Lied

She lied, looking him right in the eye in front of the whole room, happy to be destroying his life, knowing she didn't have to prove anything.

She Entered

She entered in high-heeled, confident strides, in the elegant attire of a supermodel, head held high, a suffocating trail of cigarette smoke wafting behind her.

Across the Room

Across the room from me, on the couch, she leaned to her right, rested an elbow on the armrest, crossed her legs at the knees, and batted her eyes towards me, probably hoping I wouldn't see her as the snake that she was.

Her Rain-Soaked Dress

Her rain-soaked dress clinging to her hardened dark nipples, she stood at my doorstep at two in the morning, claiming her husband was out of town and she was afraid of thunder and lightning.

For a Moment

For a moment, in total silence, the little girl scowled at her aunt's bare feet before looking up and asking, "Are you a boy or a girl?"

He Had Reached an Age

He had reached an age in which his back had a permanent forward tilt at the waistline, his knees no longer fully straightened when he walked, and erections without pharmaceutical intervention were a distant and fading memory.

Chewing Gum

Chewing gum, lips apart, upper lip curled upwards on the left side, he slouched in the driver's seat, one arm dangling through the open window, convinced the girls would notice and want him.

That Night at the Dinner Table

That night at the dinner table, the same table on which just a few hours ago he'd rocked her to the screaming throes of passion, he sat, holding a steak knife in one hand, wishing he could slice her throat.

The Day She'd Always Dreaded

The day she'd always dreaded came on their sixteenth wedding anniversary, which was also the girl's sixteenth birthday—the day the DNA results arrived in the mail.

She First Caught My Eye

She first caught my eye on the cover of a magazine, not the kind that features celebrity bimbos but esteemed academics.

He'd Always Believed

He'd always believed that chicks on social media were not for dating but for looking at, the same way you'd walk through an art gallery or a zoo.

She Walked In

She walked in, hips swinging, eyelashes fluttering, her discount fake lips—common in many areas of Miami—clamoring for attention.

In a Mild Sweat

In a mild sweat, she stood in the middle of the store, gripping the shopping cart in front of her, a frown on her face, realizing that she had no idea where the suppositories were located, and there was no way in hell she was going to ask for help.

I'm Not Husband Material

I'm not husband material. I'm the guy wives call when their husbands aren't enough—when wives crave an afternoon of slutty, froth-filled sexual filth.

At the Book Fair

At the book fair, in the middle of paging through yellowed pages with library smells that took her back to her childhood, somewhere in the throng of used book buyers, she felt him staring at her, seeing her without being seen by her. She wondered how old he would be by now.

She Opened Her Eyes

She opened her eyes and pulled her blankets halfway up her face as the footsteps in the hallway grew closer, reminding her of what had happened last time.

While Gardening

While gardening in her backyard, she happened to look up, straight through the gap in the wall, into her neighbor's yard, where two stray dogs were doing something she hadn't done in five years.

Peering Through the Window

Peering through the window, they saw withered, flailing tits as she straddled and bounced on a giant dildo. Immediately, they understood why Grandma had not been answering her phone.

I Will Die as I Have Lived

I will die as I have lived—alone, remembered, and honored by only a few people who called me "Sir."

My Ideal Woman

My ideal woman has the dignity and eloquence of royalty and the sexual deviance of a crack whore.

Under the Stars

Under the stars, on a moonlit night, she came to the garden alone to come with me in the shadows.

Love Shouldn't Hurt

Love shouldn't hurt, but it did, and she loved it.

Having Been Repeatedly Warned

Having been repeatedly warned by our parents to never go near the abandoned house, my friends and I took the first opportunity to go *inside* the abandoned house.

The Hike Into the Woods

The hike into the woods had been to take some modeling pictures for social media, and that's what it turned out to be—initially.

Alone, Lonely, and Pregnant

Alone, lonely, and pregnant, she wondered who the father might be; there was also the matter of breaking the news to her virgin fiancé.

They Sat on Opposite Ends

They sat on opposite ends of the couch, bodies angled away from each other, both determined to not be the first to speak or look at the other. In a cramped apartment occupied by two people in what is supposed to be an exclusive and committed relationship, used condoms don't just appear without the knowledge of at least one of the occupants.

Her Day

Her day, gray and devoid of sunshine, began with a loud smack across her face as her toddler announced his need to poop. She opened her eyes, rubbed her face, and contemplated the consequences of going back to sleep. Reason told her to get up; her body said otherwise, and her eyelids chose to get some rest. The second smack across her face convinced her body to agree with reason. She opened her eyes, rubbed her face, and for a moment—a very brief moment—she contemplated the merits of filicide.

At the End of the Day

At the end of the day—the most depressing part for him—not yet ready to head home, he'd sit in the parking lot, hands on the steering wheel, watching his coworkers walk out of the brick office building—some in twos or threes, others alone—and he'd wonder how many of them hated their spouses.

One Day

One day, I walked into the men's room at the mall, and a man with tired eyelids, red streaks in his eyeballs, and bags under his eyes asked me if I was married. When I informed him that I wasn't, he told me that if a woman ever expressed an interest in marrying me, I should kill her. He washed his hands, dried them on his pants, and vanished.

Shortly After Midnight

Shortly after midnight, in her heavy, full-length black coat, hands deep in her pockets, her face tense from the biting cold, she stood away from the street lights, just a few steps into the alley, in the shadow of the building, watching cars slowly drive by, the reflections of their headlights sliding along the surface of the wet road.

In the Bathroom

In the bathroom, hiding from her husband, her neck craned forward as her frown deepened. She slid her glasses down the bridge of her nose, examining the document more closely, suddenly realizing what her husband had done.

Lost in Thought

Lost in thought, she leaned back, one arm resting on the desk as she twirled and spun a yellow pencil between her fingers. Occasionally, she poked the eraser end of the pencil against her cheek as if to activate more powerful thinking powers.

Using Both Hands

Using both hands, as if the gravity of the situation demanded it, he removed his glasses, his eyes never leaving the lifeless body he'd just found in his office.

The Girl

In front of the room, the girl, no more than eight years old, tilted her head over her left shoulder, shrugged, palms facing up, and told her class she had no idea why her mother called her father the Jack Hammer of Hamilton.

The Look on His Face

The look on his face, making it clear he wasn't going to say a word, told her he didn't believe a word she'd said. For that, she hated him even more. Just once, she would have loved to have her intricately woven tapestry of lies trigger a verbal response instead of making her feel like she'd lost an argument without him saying a word.

He'd Sent All

He'd sent all of his employees home early, and now, with his hands on the back of his head, fingers interlocked, he paced from one end of his expansive office to the other. The solution was clear: just one more gamble, a good one, and everything would straighten out. He returned to his desk and sat hunched over, forehead nested in the palm of one clammy hand, an iPad in the other. Just one more bet. Just one good one.

He Decided

He decided to wear soft shoes with soft soles that don't make a sound when a man approaches a woman from behind. That night, in the moonlight, he emerged from the shadows and made his way to the window he'd pried open earlier in the day. Quietly, he opened the window, crawled in, took one step, and the damn shoes squeaked.

On Her First Day

On her first day as a new employee and head of her department, she stood in the conference room, facing her subordinates. She knew every single one of them had been with the company for over a decade; all had applied for her job, and all wanted her to fail.

The Answer Finally Came

The answer finally came to her, not while doing painstaking research online, but as she chewed her fingernails while gazing through the window, watching the clouds float by.

Unconcerned

Unconcerned, the boy feigned surprise and confusion, feeling sure no one would look in his back pocket for the missing chocolate chip cookies. Things changed when he was invited to sit on the wooden chair beside his father.

Her Chin

Her chin cradled between her thumb and index finger, she waited, unblinking, ready to pounce on the next lie that came out of his mouth.

The Cashier

The day she smiled at me was the day I opened my heart to her, allowing her madness into my world. Many a time, I had told myself that the right woman would find me. She'd fall right onto my lap, out of the sky, bringing untold wonders into my life.

It all started as I stood in the grocery store checkout lane, oblivious to my surroundings, shuffling along as the woman in front of me moved forward. If I hadn't become engrossed in some news story on my phone, I'd have heard how the conversation started. Instead, all I heard amid the grocery store murmur was, "Right?"

"Right?" This time, the voice was louder.

I looked up to find the checkout girl and the woman she was helping both looking at me with curious anticipation.

"Right? Don't you agree?" asked the cashier again.

I looked at her, then at the customer, before turning back to the cashier. "Don't I agree with what?"

"Women are crazy, right?" asked the cashier, handing the customer her change and receipt.

My eyes darted between the two of them, knowing that the correct answer was probably some politically correct fluff. The customer picked up her grocery bags, turned towards me, raised her eyebrows, and tightened her lips as if to say, "I'm staying the heck out of this one." Then, she slinked away.

I moved forward, placed my milk and loaf of bread on the counter, and waited.

"Women are crazy, right?" Her brown eyes dug into mine as she asked.

"You don't look familiar. Are you new here? I shop here all the time."

"This is my…" She tilted her head and looked away in thought. "It's been almost a week, I think, probably five or so days."

"Ah, I see." I nodded, smiling because I'd managed to change the subject.

"Women are crazy, right?"

I took a deep breath. "Well, some are," I finally said.

"But most women are crazy, right?" She swiped the bread over the scanner. Nothing happened.

"Not the ones I've known. At least, not when they're with me."

"So, you know how to set a woman straight?" She smiled at me, swiping the bread over the scanner a few more times.

I'm pretty sure it was that smile, but it could have been my inner idiot deciding to come out and play, "Sure, I know how to set a woman straight."

"Do you think I'm crazy?" She asked, finally getting a beep from the bread's barcode.

The next words out of my mouth would either be a step up or an implosion. Fortunately, before I could answer, she continued.

"Do you think you could set me straight?" She reached for the milk.

"More than likely," I said, a smirk on my face. "There's only one way to find out."

"Maybe we'll just have to find out, then." The milk was scanned without any problems.

I walked out of that store with a smile on my face, a bounce in my step, and anticipation in other places.

The following Saturday, I stood in front of the kitchen sink, looking through the window, enjoying the sight and sounds of the pouring rain in my backyard. I wondered how much longer it would be before she'd arrive, what she'd be wearing, and what squirrels did when it rained like this.

Alone Inside the Elevator

Alone inside the elevator, eyes focused on the floor indicator above the door, he watched the numbers change, his heart beating faster with each ascent. Poised, determined, and sweating like an old man in a sauna, he dug his hands into his pockets to wipe them dry.

Left Speechless

Left speechless, perplexed by his statement, a deep crevice formed between her eyebrows. Her lips, pursed, wrinkled, and slightly apart, quivered ever so slightly.

In the Moments That Followed

In the moments that followed, she sat staring at the text, struggling to hide her emotions, realizing that if she blinked, her tears would drip onto her desk.

As They Sat Side by Side

As they sat side by side in front of the laptop, realizing that poverty had just made a turn into their driveway, she wondered whether she should tell him about her secret bank account or pack her bags and wish him well.

When She Yelped

When she yelped like a puppy falling off a couch, her two coworkers looked over. They found her covering her mouth with both hands, a widened glare in her eyes as she looked at her computer screen. Both coworkers, without standing up or saying a word, slowly rolled their chairs to her desk. For what seemed like forever, not a word was spoken, and no eye contact was made. All they could do was stare at the screen.

She Couldn't Decide

His smile, revealing just his two top front teeth as his mustache curled over his upper lip, could have been disarming or alarming. She wasn't sure which.

Even Though

Even though no one ever talked to her at work, she knew enough about everyone's business to bring them down—all of them, every single one of them.

He Looked at the Clock

He looked at the clock on the wall inside his office, wondering why his supervisors had insisted on placing it there on his day off. Was this just a case of paranoia, or was he being reasonable? He hadn't skipped his medications, so he was probably being reasonable. Maybe if he were to skip his medications, he might get some better insight.

Standing Inside Her Closet

Standing inside her closet, trying to decide what to wear for the big date, she tapped her finger over her lips, the way she often did when in deep thought. That was when she felt it—the beginning of a cold sore.

He Stood at the Entrance

He stood at the entrance of the grocery store aisle, scratching his head where it had no itch, trying to remember what his wife had sent him to get.

Away From Her Desk

Away from her desk, she sat on the floor, leaning against the wall, balancing a cold drink on one bent knee, telling herself that alcohol made her more creative and she could stop drinking at any time.

Eyes Closed

Eyes closed, he rubbed his forehead with his hand, ran his hand over his scalp—all the way to the back and then back to the front—and then opened his eyes. His wife was still there, on top of the covers, face up, naked, and dead.

The Last Time

The last time I'd seen him, he'd been a silhouette in the middle of the night, on the far side of the alley, running, his trench coat flapping behind him like a cape. Now, here I was, the man he thought he'd killed, looking him dead in the eye.

On a Beautiful Spring Day

On a beautiful spring day, I drove the entire length of Mount Vernon Road, hoping to see a mountain named Vernon. I saw no such thing—stupid Americans.

Rushing to Work

Rushing to work, three hours after she should have been there, she remembered that on the previous day, she'd used her employer's copy machine to make copies of her résumé and forgotten the master copy and all the copies on the machine.

A Simple and Shallow Man

I asked, "Do you ever wear any makeup?"

The look on her face made it clear that wasn't the response she'd been expecting. "Do I ever wear any makeup?" she asked. "Is that what you just asked me?"

"Yes, that's what I asked."

Her response wasn't quite a huff, nor was it a puff. Had some breath come out, it could have qualified as a sigh. Instead, her mouth opened, and her chest appeared to sink in, as if breathing out, but I'm convinced no breath came out. "You'll only accompany me if I wear some makeup?"

"That's not what I said."

With the voice and facial expression of someone who'd just finished a marathon, she asked, "You just asked me whether or not I ever wear any makeup, right?"

"That's right."

"So, if whether or not I wear any makeup doesn't matter, why are you asking?"

"I didn't say it doesn't matter."

She lowered her face as her eyebrows rose while maintaining eye contact. "So, you do want me to wear makeup?"

"That's not what I said."

"What?"

"In all the time I've seen you here." I gestured towards the food court. "I've never seen you wearing any makeup. Given that you're always here on your lunch break from work, I know you don't wear makeup when you go to work. I wondered whether you did things differently when you were not at work."

She looked away, then back at me as she processed my response. "So, you're saying it doesn't matter to you whether or not I wear makeup?"

"Oh, no, it matters to me—greatly."

"What?" Slightly, she pushed away her styrofoam food container.

"It's just that I would prefer that you not wear any makeup."

"What? Why?"

"Because I'm a simple and shallow man."

"A simple and shallow man," she repeated. "What makes you a simple and shallow man?"

"I enjoy being in the company of a pretty woman."

She looked around the food court before gesturing with her right hand, starting from her left shoulder and spanning the entire food court. "Look around you. Look at all these pretty women. All of them are wearing makeup. Are they not pretty to you?"

"How do you know they're pretty?" I asked.

"I'm looking at them. Aren't they pretty to you?" She appeared to be genuinely confused.

"Their makeup's pretty. I've no idea what they look like. We've seen most of these people before. They're here when we are. We've no idea what they look like when they're not wearing any makeup. Do you think you know what they look like without their slathered-up fake faces?"

She looked around the food court again. I guessed she was trying to imagine each woman without any makeup. "Have you always had something against dating women who wear makeup?"

"Oh, so, this is a date? When you asked me to accompany you, that's not the assumption I made." I pulled out my phone. "Let me just update this group chat. I've family members who'll be thrilled to know that I have a date coming up."

"You know what I mean," she said, rolling her eyes. "What's with you and women wearing makeup? They do it for men, you know. The whole beauty industry prospers from the faces of brainwashed women."

"You're so right. There are women out there who'd rather die than venture into a grocery store while not wearing any makeup."

"Kinda sad when you think about it." She paused. "How did this righteous stand against makeup begin? Have you always been like this? "

"Nope, I haven't. It's something that happened after some incidents."

"Incidents? What incidents were those?"

"Have you ever dated women?"

"No, I haven't."

"Well, I have. You see that woman over there?" I pointed to a group of people standing in line, waiting to place their orders.

"The one with the nice butt? She's pretty."

"That's the one. I knew a woman like that once—she looked just like her. I knew her for a while. Every time I saw her, she looked just like that." I nodded towards the woman with the nice butt. "Then, one day, she spent the night. Now, I don't pray that much, but the next morning, I had to pray."

"You had to pray *after* getting her to spend the night?"

Nodding, I continued. "I walked into the bathroom just as she stepped out of the shower. With all that makeup gone from her face, I had to pray." I raised my hands up towards the ceiling. "I had to pray and ask for a way out of that predicament."

"That bad, huh?"

"That bad."

"One bad incident, and you swore off all women who wear makeup?"

"No, no, it wasn't just one incident. There were enough to give me a psychiatric diagnosis."

"And what diagnosis was that?"

"Post-traumatic stress disorder."

"I'm so disgusted by you," she said, breathless with laughter.

She Stood Next to Her Father

She stood next to her ninety-year-old father, her arm around his shoulders, as he stared emotionless at the food in front of him. Leaning over to look at his face, she rubbed his back and asked if he wanted something else to eat. That was when she noticed the tears.

In Shorts

In shorts and an undersized T-shirt, she sat at the end of the pier, dangling her legs over the edge, the roughness of the peeling old wood pressed against the back of her thighs. Closing her eyes, she leaned back, balancing herself with her hands behind her body, listening to the birds in the trees—her mind serene, oblivious of the eyes watching her from just beyond the woodline.

She Drove Home

She drove home, dreading the crisis that awaited her, knowing exactly how anything she said would be responded to. When she arrived, she found her eighteen-year-old son sitting in the dining room, elbows on the table, hands repeatedly rubbing his face. When she spoke to him, he looked up before immediately getting up, turning, and leaving the room. She called out to him, unsure about how to handle the situation. He continued to walk away, drifting further down the hallway. She called out again. This time, he swung around and rapidly stomped back towards her, jabbing his finger towards her as he walked.

"What?" he yelled. "What do you want from me?" Boiling anger and frustration were apparent on his face.

"I just thought you might want to talk..." Her voice, soft, almost timid, trailed off.

"Talk?" He waved his arms in the air. "To you?"

"I thought that maybe..."

"Maybe what? Maybe you could comfort me by telling me everything will be okay? Okay, fine! Let's talk. She cheated on me. Okay? She cheated on me the same way you cheated on Dad." He paused. "There, I said it. Now, what? Make that feel better! Can you?"

From the Way He Looked at Her

From the way he looked at her after all the guests had left, she knew she was in trouble. With just the two of them in a house so big and so remote, not a soul would hear her scream. She knew that look, knew what it meant, and knew what was coming. When he began walking towards her, she knew that trouble had begun. It was the good kind of trouble—the kind that makes a woman scream.

Alone in the Woods

Alone in the woods, surrounded by the smell of nature, she sat alone where the thick roots, growing horizontally, had been exposed by erosion. This was her sanctuary, where she came to be alone with her thoughts, strategizing how she might, if she could, end the world.

In the Darkness

In the darkness and silence of her upstairs bedroom, in the dead of night, the moon reflecting off her face, she stood by the window looking skywards. At that moment, from the corner of her eye, she caught a movement in her backyard. In the shadows, where patches of moonlight shot through the trees, she saw, without a doubt in her mind, a man.

The Man

The man, his face a picture of hunger, agony, and homelessness, limped into the medical office. His clothing, jeans and a denim jacket, in multiple random places, looked as if globs of automotive grease had soaked into the fabric. On his left foot, he wore a tattered shoe; his other shoe he held with both hands in front of him. Gingerly, he placed his right foot, bare and swollen, on its outer edge as he walked. With each step, his toes spread and twitched in apparent pain.

Noticing the man, the lady at the front desk, her face layered with makeup and an overly generous fragrance coating the air around her, stood up, went around her desk, and approached him.

With one hand on her hip, the other waving in front of the man, she said, "This is not a free clinic. You have to leave."

The Streets

By the time she clocked out of her dishwashing job, the streets, now deserted, were bathed in a yellowish-orange glow from the streetlights.

Walking alone, as she always did, her whole body ached from being on her feet all shift, hauling loads of dirty dishes. Occasionally, she looked up at the dark windows of the apartments adjacent to the road, thinking, with envy, about the lives of the people within. Unlike her, they were able to be home early, go to bed early, and know what it was like to actually rest. They all went to bed early, it seemed—all except the face on the third floor of the fourth building on the right.

For a while now, she'd been seeing the face on the window, watching her as she walked home. Lately, the person had started to wave at her as she walked by. The first time it happened, she wasn't sure how to respond but decided that the polite thing to do would be to wave back. She waved back, though timidly, and nobody died. So, in the days that followed, she waved some more, a bit more freely, then with some enthusiasm, ultimately finding herself looking forward to the wave. The face on the window became a guardian angel of sorts. It was, therefore, with great enthusiasm that, once again, she approached the fourth building on the right, stretching her neck, hoping for the face and the wave.

To her surprise and disappointment, no face awaited her on the third floor of the fourth building on the right. For a moment, even though she decided that it made no sense, a feeling of abandonment engulfed her. Then, while still looking at that third-floor window as she approached the fourth building, a movement caught her eyes. At the entrance of the building—the fourth building on the right—a shadowy figure appeared. It was a man, a tall and wide man, looking at her. Was this the man with the face?

Suddenly, gone was all the eagerness she'd ever felt for the face and the wave.

I Awake

I awake thinking of last night, look at the clock, and realize it's still tonight. Only twenty minutes have passed since the girls left, only twenty minutes since I said I'd think it over. I roll over between the sheets, where their scents, exotic and from far away, still linger.

I toss; I turn; I turn the lights on.

Reaching for my laptop on the nightstand, I wonder what keywords would be best. "Donating sperm to lesbian couple" sounds precise.

Ever So Slightly

Ever so slightly, I crack open the back door, and the wind howls at me, trees sway in the distance, and the dark sky flashes a warning. Thunder cracks, the heavens open, and the torrent begins. Usually, from the safety of my home, I cherish such moments. Today is not one of those days. Against my advice, she's out there, somewhere, battling the elements, determined to fight her way through a three-hour drive to be with me. Her cell phone, perhaps a victim of the angry skies, has been unreachable. With heaviness in my chest and a weakness I can barely control, I click the door shut.

On the couch, chest heaving, I slouch, trying to control my breath. Through the windows, I see the outside has become darker as the sun has set, and louder as the cascade increases. I close my eyes to avoid the darkness.

In my mind's eye, I see her. She's driving in the middle of Dead Man's Curves, a narrow two-lane, two-mile stretch snaking its way through the mountains—a vertical incline on the left and a mile-long straight drop on the right. And then, she's no longer on Dead Man's

Curves. She's over the edge, her car in midair, spinning.

Startled, I awake. It's the doorbell. I make my way to the door, wondering if it's her or first responders here to tell me she's been found. Just as I reach for the door, I remember something. She has a key. Why would she ring the doorbell?

Her Spindly Legs

Her spindly legs were in black, heavy, lace-up, mid-calf boots and tiny denim shorts with frayed bottom edges. The T-shirt she wore, white and trimmed to reveal her midsection, had short sleeves, exposing arms that curved inward like a newborn's legs. The makeup, consisting of black lipstick and black circles around eyes with extended black eyelashes, was meant to go with the black electric guitar propped against her crotch—a guitar she had no idea how to play.

In a Crowd

In a crowd clad in sweatpants, jeans, and an assortment of fluffy jackets, he stood out. This was a man in a knee-length black coat, a formal gray hat, and a blue shirt with a tie in a different shade of blue. His gray pants, made from a fabric that made her want to reach out and caress his legs, had creases, indicating that someone had taken the time to iron them. On his feet, black shoes, polished to a reflective shine. When taking pictures, he used a real camera with an adjustable lens, not a cell phone. She had to find out more about him.

Forceful and Unrelenting

Forceful and unrelenting, the gusts of wind, whooping, whooshing, and howling, slam her car in irregular waves. The windshield wipers, as well as the headlights, begin to lose the battle against the downpour. Her hands ache from how tightly she grips the steering wheel. Her teeth, every single one of them, ache from the heavy clenching of her jaws. Barely making contact with the accelerator, her right foot quivers, causing her whole leg to shake as the car, sliding along, slowly weaves from side to side on the narrow two-lane stretch of Dead Man's Curves.

Continuing to drive is a bad gamble, and hitting the brakes would be an even bigger one. The only choice is hope. She's seen Dead Man's Curves on a clear day. She knows about the mile-long vertical drop just steps away from her car. If she can just come to a stop, maybe she can wait out the worst part. Just then, not too far ahead of her, swaying from side to side, appearing out of control, are headlights heading in her direction.

Perched on the Couch

Perched on the couch's armrest, her thighs drawn up against her chest, arms hugging her legs, she rested her chin on her knees. With the TV now muted, she continued to listen to the raised voices from the apartment next door.

"I warned you. I knew you wouldn't like the reason. Now, you're mad at me," he said.

"You're basically calling me stupid," she responded.

"When did I say you were stupid? All I said was that the reason they don't pay you much is that your job can be done by just about anybody."

"It's still an important job. It takes a lot of thinking, skill, and hard work," she said.

"I don't doubt or question that at all. I've seen what you do. Like I said, maybe if you make a name for yourself, you can make more money down the road. I think there are a lot of social media managers who make a lot of money."

"You work a fraction of what I work and make ten times what I make. This whole month, you've been working four hours a day. Four hours!" The frustration in her voice could be felt through the wall. "Four hours of work and cat videos online the rest of the day!"

"Honey, I keep telling you. Your job can be done by pretty much anyone. I'm an accountant—a licensed professional. I don't have as much competition as you do. You're competing with high school dropouts. I'm not. So, I make more money."

"I'm a college graduate, too!"

"Yes, but that's irrelevant to your job. You work from home, online, doing a job that isn't that specialized and doesn't require a degree. Do you realize what that means?"

"What?"

"When you apply for a job like that, every single person on the planet who happens to have internet access is your competition, as long as they speak the language." There was some silence before he continued. "I'm sorry, but that's just the truth."

For a moment, there was some more silence, followed by sounds of someone sobbing.

In a Lonely Stretch of the Road

In a lonely stretch of the road, hours from any sign of humanity, amidst the miles of dry grass stretching towards distant woods, stood what I had come to call The Wall. It was all that was left of a stately, two-story, stone structure. The Wall stood prominent and defiant, about 100 meters from the road.

One day, as I drove by, with some time to kill, I decided to stop and take a closer look at The Wall. I stepped out of the car, the wind whistling around me. In both directions, the road—a gaping strip of emptiness—stretched into the horizon. Adjacent to the road, on both sides, not a sign of life. Nothing but grass—dry, brown, dead grass.

I eyed the three strands of rusty barbed wire I'd have to climb over, then looked all around me again. If there ever was a perfect place in which to be murdered, this would be it.

In the Corridor

In the corridor, he paced up and down, hands balled up in his pants pockets, a frown on his face, eyes never leaving the tiled floor. Oblivious to all else, he got in everyone's way as nurses scurried back and forth, tending to their patients.

One Bright and Lazy Afternoon

One bright and lazy afternoon, as the sun flooded the area with an intense wave of sweltering heat, a young lady in a stylish red dress and elegant men's shoes knocked on my door.

In the Crowd

In the crowd, side by side, each feeling lost and alone, they held hands, not because of some deep feelings of affection for each other, but because all the other couples were.

Sunday Afternoons, Towards Sunset

Sunday afternoons, towards sunset, were the worst. That's when, on the verge of tears, we had to pry ourselves from each other, shower together, and let her prepare for the overnight drive back to her husband.

We Must Have Been Around Five

We must have been around five years old when my cousin and I got married—in the brick building behind the house, where the tools were kept. Since it was just the two of us, I, as the man, served as the pastor. Immediately after the ceremony, she pulled up her dress, held it up, partially tucked under her chin, and we both gazed intently at her belly, waiting for a baby to grow.

I Sat

I sat, fearful of being disrespectful or making a fool of myself. What was in front of me was either a wooden cup with no handle or a rather small bowl. Not sure whether to drink from the container or wait for a spoon to be offered, I waited, my head and neck motionless, eyes darting furtively, hoping to catch what others were doing.

Holding a Microphone

Holding a microphone in front of her, sitting next to her husband on stage, looking down at the hall full of admirers, she wondered what her life would have been like had she married for love.

Embarrassed by Her Tears

Embarrassed by her tears and hating herself for her weakness, nothing hurt more than having to admit that she'd be wrong and he'd be right.

Alone at Home

Alone at home after school, her first mistake was thinking that no harm could come from trying on her mother's pantyhose. The second one was not removing the pantyhose when the doorbell rang.

I Drove Over the Hill

I drove over the hill, and in the distance, on the right side of the road, there it was. Greeting me was a bleak, soot-covered scattering of buildings, mostly looking like abandoned warehouses. This grand metropolis, with its tinge of gray dust hovering above it, was to be my new home. This was a place so dismal even the trees, all covered in a grayish powdery substance, looked depressed.

Marriage

"So, how come you've never been married?" she asked in the din of the food court.

"It's just my way of contributing to women's happiness."

"In what way?" The glint in her eye suggested she was sure she knew where I was going with that.

"I'm giving women, the world over, one less husband to complain about."

"Huh?"

"Isn't that the primary topic when married women get together?"

"And how are you privy to what married women talk about when they are together?"

"Let's just say I have my ways."

"Okay, fine. You have your ways. Now, what ways are those?"

"I'm a lifelong student of human behavior. That comes with a host of skills and techniques for observing humankind."

"I'm not sure I can buy any of that. You can observe humankind and somehow be able to tell what people talked about when you were not there?"

"No, no. It's not like that. Sometimes, people open up to me and tell me personal stuff. At other times, they simply talk around me, and I hear them. In other cases, I read what people write online and learn a lot from it."

"So one of your skills is eavesdropping?"

"Eavesdropping has a rather unsavory connotation. Let's just say I'm attentive to my surroundings, observant if you will, using all my senses as needed."

"And your powers of observation tell you that women complain about their husbands." She made a face. "Men complain about their wives all the time, too."

"Yes, but that's not the direction I look when the subject of marriage is brought up. You asked me why I've never been married. So, my mind immediately went to women."

"Fair enough. What can you tell me about what, as a lifelong student of human behavior, you have learned about humanity?"

"The most important thing, I think, is that human beings are not very good at being good to each other. Most of the time, humans just put up with each other because other human beings have determined that there should be negative consequences for what is deemed bad behavior."

"Interesting point. Is that what makes married women complain about their husbands?"

"One could make that argument. I'd also argue that in many marriages, spouses, in general, not just women, compete against each other instead of working together."

"Why do you think that is?"

"As human beings, we have a need to feel good about ourselves."

"That's not a bad thing, is it?"

"It's not a bad thing. What happens is that we tend to feel better about ourselves, mainly by comparing ourselves to others. Whether we're looking at our jobs, pay, houses, neighborhoods, or looks, we evaluate everything by comparing it to what others have. If we don't measure up, we start to trash others. We find fault with what other people have. That way, we fool ourselves into some feelings of superiority. That's the bad part—the part where we want to crush other people in order to feel better about our own standing."

"I've seen that happen to a lot of celebrities. That's not to say some of them don't deserve the ridicule that they get."

I nodded in agreement. "I'm also willing to bet that over the last two thousand years, maybe even more, there hasn't been a single day in which there hasn't been a war somewhere in the world. Why? Because humans plain suck at being good to each other."

"Lord, you're so depressing."

"Just answering your questions, my dear."

"Do you have other reasons for not being married?"

"Oh, yeah, I have some more."

"How many more do you have?"

"You don't have enough time to hear them all. It's time for you to head back to work. Don't keep our patients waiting."

She looked at her watch. "Maybe next time."

"Maybe next time."